THE
ATTORNEY
AND THE
Saguaro Cactus

BY AN ANONYMOUS WITNESS

MAGDALENA HESS

HESS
press

HESS

press

Copyright © 2025 by Magdalena Hess
All rights reserved.
Published by Hess Press

HESS
press

For my son,
a brilliant attorney and an even finer human being.
Thank you for filling the Arizona desert with laughter.
This story was inspired by that journey, by your presence and the joy you
brought to each moment.
In every page, there's a piece of that desert sun
and the light you shared along the way. Enduring, graceful, and rooted,

Strong like the Saguaro Cactus.

And to YOU

As you turn these pages, I hope this story stays with you.
It is about legacy, laughter, and the quiet moments that shape
who we are.
And like the Saguaro, may you stand tall in your own journey.

Once upon a time, in sunny Tucson, Arizona, a young man arrived in the desert.

He wore an elegant suit and shiny shoes, and around his neck was his papa's tie. He was an attorney who loved facts, details,

and, most of all, thinking things through.

He had come to Tucson for the Papa Awards a joyful celebration honoring his Papa, a beloved Jewelry designer with a charm that sparkled just like his designs.

The attorney, new to the desert, was dazzled.

Cacti... Coyotes... Chimichangas...

So much to see and so little sunscreen!

Excited to explore, he drove and drove down long roads and around roundabouts

that made his head spin... until he found Momo Restaurant.

It looked more like a "No-no" than a "Momo."

"Eh," he shrugged. "How bad could it be?"

Spoiler:

He never found out.

His stomach said: "yes!" But his feet seemed to say: "let's walk."

Curious, he strolled into the desert to meet the locals starting with the mighty Saguaro cactus.

"Hi, Saguaro!" he said cheerfully to the first cactus he bumped into. The huge cactus blinked down at him. "You're not as tall as me!" it said.

Then it shooed him away with a prickly pout.

So, he tried another, medium-sized cactus.

"Hi, Saguaro!" he said to the second cactus.

"Hey!" said the cactus, a little crossly.

"You're blocking my sun!"   The attorney ducked and fled.

So he tried a third, much smaller, cactus.
 "Hi, Sagu—OW!"

 He had sat on a baby saguaro!

"Ow!" squeaked the baby cactus. "I may be small, but I'm still growing here!"

The attorney jumped up, startled and a little sore.

"Oh no I'm so sorry," he said, brushing himself off. "I didn't see you there."

The baby cactus wiggled slightly, as if to say, "Maybe next time, you will."

The attorney gave it a thoughtful look. This desert really was full of surprises.

And with that, he got back into his car and drove away.

That night, at the Papa Awards, he danced.

He blew bubbles. He wore party glasses.

He tried to forget about the grumpy saguaro cacti.

But when the music stopped and he stepped outside for air... there was the first mighty saguaro cactus looking down on him again. It was BIG. It was silent. And it was very spiky. And next to him was the smaller cactus and next to him the baby cactus.

The first saguaro grabbed the attorney's tie.

HIS PAPA'S TIE!

"Let go!" he cried

"That's My Papa's Tie"

A watching lizard gasped.

A passing goat fainted.

"Wait," said the cactus, its voice deep and dry like desert wind.

"I have something to tell you."

The attorney froze.   He adjusted his glasses.

"Okay... tell me," he said, nervously.

"In life," said the tall saguaro, rather grandly, "you must stand tall. Face the world with courage. Lift your head high. Even when things feel prickly. Because when you stand tall," it added, "you help others rise, too."

Then the second saguaro cactus spoke.

"In life," it said. "You must see the bigger picture. Move out of the shade into the sun. The detail may be fascinating but the whole picture is truly beautiful."

And finally, the baby cactus spoke.

"In life," it squeaked, "we're all continually growing. Even if we may seem small on the outside, our hearts and minds are always growing."

The attorney blinked.

"That's... surprisingly wise," he said, "and kind of beautiful."

And then the attorney smiled.

 "I see now," he said. "Life isn't about proving things. It's about moving through them with courage and confidence."

The tall saguaro let go of his Papa's tie.

The lizard wiped a tear.

The goat applauded.

The Saguaros didn't speak again. They simply stood tall, bathed in moonlight.

The attorney looked out across the desert, where the stars shimmered like the

Jewelry his papa once made.

He placed a hand over his papa's tie, feeling its quiet strength.

As he turned to go, his steps felt lighter, his back stood straighter

and something inside him had shifted.

And from that day forward, whenever the attorney felt lost, low

or legally confused...

He remembered the saguaros.

"Stand tall," he would say to himself, "own your space, even when nobody understands your spikes. Step into the sun and see the big picture and," he added, "never allow your heart and mind to stop growing."

He still made mistakes of course . . .   Oops!

But he lifted his head high; walked with courage, confidence, and positivity

Strong like the Saguaro.

Because sometimes, all it takes is one spiky friend to teach you the most

human of lessons.

And sometimes you mustn't overthink. You just have to trust your gut.

(But do try not to sit on a Saguaro Cactus!)

A Note from the Desert

Often, the wisest person in the room is the one who listens. Not just with their ears, but with their heart.

Our attorney friend once trusted only what he could see and prove. But the desert had other plans offering lessons that didn't come from books, but from plants, coyotes, and a baby saguaro cactus with attitude.

You might trip over a few things. You might get a little sunburned. And sometimes, life may surprise you with something totally unexpected like a silent stare from a spiky Saguaro new friend.

That's okay.
When things feel uncertain, just pause.   Breathe.
Put a hand over your heart and feel the strength that's already there.
Because inside you is a quiet compass, a spark of knowing,

a little voice that says,

"You've got this."

xoxo

maggiehess.com

MAGDALENA HESS

Magdalena "Maggie" Hess is an award-winning jewelry designer and author.
With decades of experience crafting beauty in form, she brings that same
care to the page, offering readers stories rooted in truth, transformation,
and heartfelt reflection.
The Attorney and the Saguaro Cactus is her tribute to love, legacy, and the
power of trusting the quiet wisdom within.

HESS
press